Dear Parents:

Congratulations! Your child is taking the first steps on an exciting journey. The destination? Independent reading!

STEP INTO READING® will help your child get there. The program offers five steps to reading success. Each step includes fun stories and colorful art or photographs. In addition to original fiction and books with favorite characters, there are Step into Reading Non-Fiction Readers, Phonics Readers and Boxed Sets, Sticker Readers, and Comic Readers—a complete literacy program with something to interest every child.

Learning to Read, Step by Step!

Ready to Read   Preschool–Kindergarten
• big type and easy words • rhyme and rhythm • picture clues
For children who know the alphabet and are eager to begin reading.

Reading with Help   Preschool–Grade 1
• basic vocabulary • short sentences • simple stories
For children who recognize familiar words and sound out new words with help.

Reading on Your Own   Grades 1–3
• engaging characters • easy-to-follow plots • popular topics
For children who are ready to read on their own.

Reading Paragraphs   Grades 2–3
• challenging vocabulary • short paragraphs • exciting stories
For newly independent readers who read simple sentences with confidence.

Ready for Chapters   Grades 2–4
• chapters • longer paragraphs • full-color art
For children who want to take the plunge into chapter books but still like colorful pictures.

STEP INTO READING® is designed to give every child a successful reading experience. The grade levels are only guides; children will progress through the steps at their own speed, developing confidence in their reading.

Remember, a lifetime love of reading starts with a single step!

Visit us on the Web!
StepIntoReading.com
randomhousekids.com

Educators and librarians, for a variety of teaching tools, visit us at RHTeachersLibrarians.com

ISBN 978-1-5247-1694-3 (trade) — ISBN 978-1-5247-1695-0 (lib. bdg.)

Printed in the United States of America

10 9 8 7 6 5 4 3 2 1

STEP INTO READING®

STEP 1

READY TO READ

nickelodeon

THE SPOOKY CABIN

based on the teleplay "Pups and the
Ghost Cabin" by Scott Albert

illustrated by Jason Fruchter

Random House 🏠 New York

Jake is fixing up
an old cabin.
Rocky and Rubble
are helping him.

It is lunchtime.

Uh-oh!

Rubble's food

is gone!

Jake's lunch box floats

into the cabin.

Is a ghost

moving it?

Jake calls Ryder

for help.

Ryder and Chase
race to the cabin.

Boom!
The porch
falls down!

Rocky finds some posts
to fix the porch.
Don't lose it–reuse it!

The pups fix
the porch!

Everyone goes
inside the cabin.
It is dark and spooky.
Bats fly through
the air.

Rubble falls into
a secret door.

Rubble is missing.
Rocky thinks a ghost
grabbed him.
Ryder does not believe
in ghosts.

Outside, Chase's spy drone
flies over the cabin.

Chase sees that Rubble
is still inside the cabin.
Rubble is not alone!

In the cabin,
Ryder, Rocky, and Jake
look for Rubble.

Lights go on and off.

Paintings move.

Ryder pushes a button.

It opens

the secret door.

Rubble is free!

Rocky sees mice
on the floor.
Ryder solves
the mystery!

The cabin is not haunted.
The mice make the lights
go on and off.

The mice make
the paintings
move.
They also
tickle Rubble's
paws!

The pups build
a little cabin for the mice.
Whenever you
are in trouble,
just squeak for help!